PLENTY OF LOVE TO GO AROUND

Emma Chichester Clark

 NANCY PAULSEN BOOKS

For my young
and beautiful
grandma

NANCY PAULSEN BOOKS

an imprint of Penguin Random House LLC

375 Hudson Street

New York, NY 10014

Nancy Paulsen Books is a registered trademark of Penguin Random House LLC.

Library of Congress Cataloging-in-Publication Data is available upon request.

Manufactured in China by Toppan Leefung Printing Limited.

ISBN 978-0-399-54666-2

1 3 5 7 9 10 8 6 4 2

The art was done in watercolor and colored pencil.

I AM PLUM.

The one and only special Plum.

Emma and Rupert are my family, and I just love them.

When they say I am their **Special One**, I feel loved all over.

Sam and Gracie live next door. They are my best friends, and I am their **best one and only**.

But one day, Gracie said, "We've got a surprise for you, Plum!"

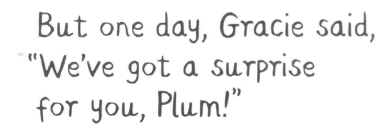

"This is Binky!"
said Sam.

He was holding
a cat.

Cats are **not** my favorite thing.

"He loves you, Plum! Don't you **LOVE** him?" asked Gracie.
"We love him!" said Sam.

I was so happy to go to the park.
The park is just for dogs.

"I say!" said my friend Esther.
"Is that cat with you?"

I couldn't believe it!

"Who's your new friend?" asked Rocket.
"He's **not** my friend!" I said.

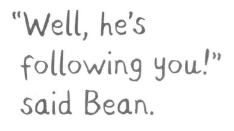

"Well, he's
following you!"
said Bean.

"Scat, cat!"
I said.

When I got home,
guess who was there?
"It's nice to have a cat
around," said Emma.

No! It isn't! It isn't!

The cat followed me everywhere,

sniffed where I sniffed,

rolled where I rolled,

peed when I peed,

stretched when
I stretched.

I couldn't
get away!

I went to the shed to hide.

But the cat followed me there too . . .

When the door slammed shut, we were stuck!

"Meow!" he said,
and off he went.

"CATS!" I said.

Now no one will
ever find me.

But I was wrong
about that, because
Binky came back with
Sam and Gracie.

"Silly Plum!"
said Gracie.

"Binky saved you!"
said Sam.

They told Emma and Rupert.
"Clever Binky!" said Rupert.

"He's SO clever!" said Sam.

He's just a CAT! Nothing special about that!

"Oh, look at Binky!" said Gracie as he ran up a tree.

"He can do **anything!**" said Sam.

It's true. It's really true, I thought.

Now Binky was the Special One.

I thought he was a **show-off**, clever-clogs cat.

"He's ruining everything!"
I told Esther.

"Have you tried
being friends?"
asked Jakey.

"I can't
be friends
with a cat!"
I told Bean.

"What if
they love him
more than me?"
I asked Rocket.

"Oh, there's plenty of love
to go around," he said.

But I wasn't sure.

Sam and Gracie were watching TV.

The cat was outside.

He came back when he saw me.

So I pushed the door shut and leaned against the cat flap.

"Stop following me!" I told him.

"Stay out till I say so."

I guarded the door. Then it started to rain. I couldn't leave him out in the rain, could I? But was there enough love to go around? Was there?

Oh, poor Binky!

Just then, Emma and Rupert came.

They found little Binky . . .

and then they saw me in front of the cat flap.

I looked at
Emma and she
looked at me.
She knew what
I'd done.

"Now, Plummie," Emma said. "You will always be my Special One . . . but you're going to **have** to be nice to the cat!

There's room in our hearts for him and for YOU!"

"You've got a big heart, haven't you, Plummie?" said Emma.

And suddenly I could feel it growing.
It grew **BIGGER** and **BIGGER**.

I have a big heart! I do. I do!
And now I know—
there's enough love for two . . .

In fact, there's PLENTY of love
to go around and around! Yes,
there's plenty of love to go around.